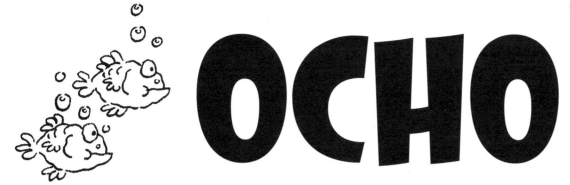

OCHO

A Character-Education Story

**WRITTEN BY
ARDEN MARTENZ**

Illustrated by Terry Sirrell

OCHO: A CHARACTER EDUCATION STORY

10-DIGIT ISBN: 1-57543-112-2
13-DIGIT ISBN: 978-1-57543-112-3

REPRINTED 2006
COPYRIGHT © 2002 MAR★CO PRODUCTS, INC.
Published by mar★co products, inc.
1443 Old York Road
Warminster, PA 18974
1-800-448-2197
www.marcoproducts.com

PRINTED IN THE U.S.A.

INTRODUCTION

Ocho is the story of an octopus who ventures into his sea community and finds his sea creature friends have changed from caring and considerate creatures to selfish and inconsiderate ones. Alarmed at the change in his community, Ocho returns to his home. There, with his cousin Ozzie, Ocho devises a plan to change his sea creature friends back to their normal selves.

This story can be presented in one or two sessions. The story and its accompanying questions and follow-up activities are appropriate for students in grades 2-4.

PRESENTING *OCHO*

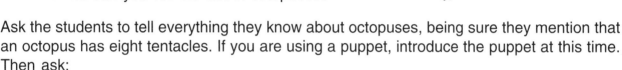

Introduce *Ocho* to the students by asking them:

"What can you tell me about octopuses?"

Ask the students to tell everything they know about octopuses, being sure they mention that an octopus has eight tentacles. If you are using a puppet, introduce the puppet at this time. Then ask:

"What other sea creatures can you name?"

Write the names of the other sea creatures on the board or overhead transparency. When the students have finished naming sea creatures, cross out the names of sea creatures that are not mentioned in the story. Add any sea creatures included in the story that the students did not mention. The list should include: clams, shrimp, seahorses, lobsters, crabs, manta rays, eels, oysters.

Tell the students:

"You are going to hear a story about an octopus named Ocho. Ocho got his name because he has eight tentacles and *ocho* means *eight* in Spanish. When I have finished reading the story, you will have learned about eight character traits and how Ocho got his friends to realize how important those qualities are."

Read the story on pages 4-27. (If you are presenting the story in two sessions read only Chapter 1.)

Review the Discussion Questions (page 28) with the students. If you are presenting the story in two sessions, ask the students questions 1-5 after reading Chapter 1. Then choose one or more of the Follow-Up Activities (pages 28-32) to reinforce the lesson. Character Wordman (page 28) and Tic-Tac Character (page 29) are classroom games that can be presented after either Chapter 1 or Chapter 2 and played by following the directions written on the activity pages. Sea Creature Character Traits (page 30), Ocho's Special Tentacles (page 31), and Ocho's Wordfind (page 32) require the leader to reproduce a copy for each student before beginning the lesson. These activities should be presented only after reading Chapter 2.

OCHO

~ CHAPTER 1 ~

Ocho is an octopus who lives at the bottom of the ocean. He loves the beautiful coral, the sea plants, and the other sea creatures that make up his world. To him, the bottom of the sea is the most wonderful place in the world to live.

One fine day, Ocho decided he would venture out to see what the other sea creatures were doing. He wondered how his friends—the seahorses, shrimp, crabs, oysters, clams, manta rays, lobsters, and eels—were doing. It had been awhile since Ocho had left his underwater cave home, and he thought he had better check to see if everything was all right.

Ocho stretched his tentacles and began to crawl along the ocean floor. For those of you who do not know about octopuses, they have both a long- and short-term memory. This means they can remember things that happened to them a little while ago or a long time before. Ocho's memory is what makes it possible for this story to take place.

As Ocho moved along the ocean floor, he saw things happening that were different from what he remembered. The sea creatures were not acting like they had acted before.

5

As Ocho glided over to Clara Clam, she snapped her shell shut. Ocho called to her, but she didn't answer. "Clara, it's me, Ocho! What's wrong? Are you all right?" No sound came from Clara. Not wanting to give up, Ocho tapped on Clara's shell, "Clara, what is going on? Answer me."

"Mind your own business!" Clara snapped, not opening her shell. "I'm sick of always being the one people run to when they have a problem. No one ever wants to listen to my problems. Just last week, I really needed a friend. But did anyone care? Would anyone listen to me? No! So now I've decided it's time everyone started handling their own problems."

Ocho was really confused. Clara Clam was one of the most caring creatures he had ever known. She was always ready to help anyone who needed a friend. If someone had a problem, Clara was there to listen and show that she cared. Now here she was with her shell closed, telling Ocho she wasn't going to be helpful any longer. "She must really be having a bad day," thought Ocho. "I guess I'd better leave her alone for now."

So Ocho moved on ...

As he moved along the ocean floor, Ocho came upon a group of seahorses. One of them was Sally Seahorse. Ocho had known Sally for a long time. Sally was a seahorse who shared with everyone. If Sally had something someone else could use, she was always happy to share. But the seahorse Ocho saw now was definitely not the Sally Seahorse he knew.

Sally was clutching a tiny sea plant and telling the other seahorses that it was hers and they had better stay away from it. Ocho had just started to talk with the seahorses when Sally said, "Mind you own business, Ocho! This is my plant, and it's going to stay mine. So just crawl away from here and leave me alone. I'm sick of sharing all the time. The other day, I really wanted a piece of Soroya's sea plant, and she just swam away. And after all the times I've shared with her! Never again! I'm keeping what I have to myself."

"Wow!" thought Ocho. "First Clara Clam was having a bad day. Now Sally's having a bad day, too. I guess I'd better leave her alone for now."

So Ocho moved on ...

As Ocho moved across the bottom of the ocean, he looked at all the wonderful things that grew there. "What beautiful plants," thought Ocho. "I love to watch them move in the water. This really is a peaceful place." Suddenly, Ocho was startled by a loud noise.

"Get out of here! This is my territory!" an angry voice bellowed.

"You're not the only one who lives here. And who do you think you are, bossing me around?" answered the second angry voice.

"What in the world is going on?" thought Ocho. "This is where Craig Crab lives, and he would never talk like that to anyone." Ocho carefully made his way through the plants. Then he saw something he'd never thought he'd see: Craig and Carl Crab screaming at each other.

Craig and Carl were twins, and they were always together. They liked the same things and, because of that, they always agreed. Ocho stared in amazement. He couldn't believe what he was seeing and hearing. "Craig! Carl! What are you doing?" Ocho asked.

"Keep out of this, Ocho," said Craig. "This is none of your business, so just crawl off," yelled Carl.

"Okay, okay," said Ocho. "Don't start yelling at me."

"Just mind your own business, and everything will be okay. And as for you, Carl," screamed Craig, "get your claws off my property and don't ever touch anything of mine again. Last week, you lied to me. You took my shell collection and you know it."

"Whatever you say, you Kooky Crab," answered Carl. "I never took your old shell collection. But if you want to think I did, it's okay with me. And what goes for me, goes for you. If I ever see you touching anything of mine, you'll be cracked crab. Understand?"

"They must be having a bad day, like Clara Clam and Sally Seahorse," thought Ocho. "I guess I'd better leave them alone for now."

So Ocho moved on ...

Ocho was glad to get away from the crab twins. They were just too angry to deal with. A little farther ahead, Ocho saw Serena Shrimp. She and her mother were looking for food, or at least that's what Ocho thought they were doing. As he moved closer to the two shrimp, he heard Serena say, "I won't, and you can't make me! Nobody else has to do what you make *me* do."

Ocho stopped. This didn't sound like Serena, talking back to her mother. Serena always respected her elders. Ocho looked at Serena's mother. He could tell that she was very upset at the way Serena was talking to her. Just then, Serena's mother scolded Serena and told her to go back to their home. Serena screamed, "I hate you! I hate you!" as she crawled off.

"Wow!" thought Ocho. "Clara Clam, Sally Seahorse, and Carl and Craig Crab are having a bad day. And Serena Shrimp and her mother are having a bad day, too! I guess I'd better leave them alone for now."

So Ocho moved on ...

MAR★CO PRODUCTS, INC. © 2002 1-800-448-2197

"This day has got to get better," thought Ocho. "These sea creatures have always been my friends, but today it's as if I have never known them. Everyone can't be having problems."

As Ocho moved on slowly, he put what he had seen behind him. He decided to crawl over to Larry Lobster's house. Larry was one of the most capable lobsters Ocho had ever known. Surely Larry could tell him what was happening.

But before Ocho could reach Larry Lobster's house, Marissa Manta swam past him. Marissa was swimming swiftly, but Ocho could see tears in her eyes. "Oh, no," thought Ocho. "What now? What could make Marissa so sad? She's usually the most playful sea creature around."

"Wait up, Marissa," called Ocho. Marissa turned around and moved her body so she would stay in one place. "What's wrong?" asked Ocho.

"It's Mandy," cried Marissa. "She told me the biggest lie. We were supposed to go swimming together yesterday. But when I went to meet her, she wasn't there. Her mother said she had gone over to Melinda's and wouldn't be back until after dark."

"Maybe she forgot she made plans with you," Ocho said, trying to make Marissa feel better. "Have you given Mandy a chance to explain why she didn't meet you?"

"No way, Ocho! If Mandy doesn't want me for a friend, that's fine with me. I'm never talking to her again!"

"I can see you're really having a bad day," said Ocho.

"You're right, Ocho," said Marissa, "I just want to be left alone."

So Ocho moved on ...

Ocho could hardly wait to get to Larry Lobster's house. The sadness and anger felt by Clara Clam, Sally Seahorse, Carl and Craig Crab, Serena Shrimp and Marissa Manta was getting to be too much for him. He needed to see and hear someone who would make him laugh.

On the way to Larry Lobster's house, Ocho had to cross the giant oyster beds. This was ordinarily an easy task, but Ocho soon found out it would not be an easy task on this day.

Ocho couldn't be sure, but it looked like the oysters were having some sort of trial. All of the oysters were gathered around a mussel. "How did a mussel get into the oyster beds?" wondered Ocho. "I wouldn't think it would make any difference, but those oysters are really making a fuss." As Ocho neared the oyster beds, the clamor became louder. He was soon able to hear what was happening.

"What do you mean, bringing a mussel home to play?" asked one of the oysters. "Mussels are mussels and oysters are oysters. We don't mix."

The little oyster and the little mussel looked frightened. They didn't know what was going to happen to them. The little oyster tried to explain that he and the mussel had met at school and were friends. They played together all the time at school and they wanted to play together after school.

But the little oyster was interrupted every time he tried to speak. The other oysters weren't interested in what he had to say. They did not want anything that was different from them in their territory. The little mussel didn't say a word. He just wanted to get away, and he wanted to get away fast.

Ocho was overwhelmed. He had never seen such an act of prejudice in his sea community. Everyone usually accepted everyone else and got along.

"I really need to get to Larry Lobster's," Ocho thought, "and it looks like I need to get there fast."

So Ocho moved on ...

Ocho had almost reached his destination when Elmer Eel swam up beside him. "Hi, Ocho! Long time, no see," Elmer said. "Where are you going?"

"I'm headed for Larry Lobster's house," said Ocho. "How have you been?"

"Better, now that I found this," answered Elmer.

"What do you have there?" asked Ocho.

"I found it this morning. It's a gold chain. See how I have wrapped it around my body? Pretty neat, huh?" boasted Elmer.

"Do you know who it belongs to?" asked Ocho.

"Sure, but finders keepers. If Eleanor Eel was dumb enough to let this slip off her body, then she deserves not to get it back. Her bad luck is my good luck," said Elmer.

At this point, Ocho didn't know whether to tell Elmer that what he was doing was wrong or just let it go. The day had been so mixed up that Ocho felt like a stranger in his own community. When he finally decided to say something to Elmer, it was too late. Elmer was gone, and all Ocho could think of was hurrying to see Larry Lobster. If Larry was acting like Clara Clam, Sally Seahorse, Carl and Craig Crab, Serena Shrimp, Marissa Manta, the oysters, and Elmer Eel, Ocho was really going to be confused!

So Ocho moved on ...

Ocho climbed over rocks until he noticed the pile of rocks that Larry Lobster called home. "At last!" Ocho thought. "At last, I'm going to find out what is going on." As Ocho approached the pile of rocks, he spied Larry lying on top of one, doing nothing. "Oh my!" thought Ocho. "It's not like Larry to do nothing, and one look at his house tells me he has been doing nothing for some time." There was litter everywhere, and Larry didn't seem to care.

"Larry," called Ocho, "it's me, Ocho. What in the world are you doing?"

"Doing?" answered Larry. "Nothing! I'm doing nothing."

"But why?" asked Ocho.

"Why? Because I don't want to do anything. That's why."

"But your house is a mess, and you look like you haven't been eating," explained Ocho.

"So? What of it? I'm tired of being the one who is responsible for everything." Larry said. "When the sea creatures elected me head of the sea community, I tried to help everyone. In the beginning, everything went well. But everyone has changed. Now, no one appreciates what I do. I tried and tried. Finally, I decided that if they didn't appreciate what I was trying to do, I would do nothing."

"But, Larry, have you seen what it's like out there?" asked Ocho.

"Sure. And frankly, I don't care."

Ocho couldn't believe what he was hearing. Larry, the most responsible of all the sea creatures, had given up. When he gave up, everyone else did, too.

"This is really a mess," thought Ocho. "I need to get home and see what I can do to get things back to normal."

So Ocho swam back home as fast as he could ...

MAR★CO PRODUCTS, INC. © 2002 1-800-448-2197

Ocho curled up in his rock cave and thought about what he had seen in the sea community.

This was his home. These were his friends. The more Ocho thought about it, the sadder and more dejected he became. He sank deeper and deeper into depression.

"What are you doing?" called a voice from outside the rock cave. "Ocho Octopus, you come out here this minute. And I do mean this *minute!*"

Ocho opened his sleepy eyes, stretched his tentacles, and slowly crawled out to see who was demanding his presence. When he reached the outside of the rock cave, he saw his cousin, Ozzie.

Ozzie lived in another sea community and didn't visit often. Ocho knew that if Ozzie had come so far to see him, it must be for an important reason.

"What do you mean, what am I doing?" asked Ocho.

"Just that," answered Ozzie. "What are you doing, and what is going on in your sea community?"

"I wish I knew. I really do wish I knew," said Ocho. "A while ago, I went out to see my friends. They had changed so much, I hardly knew them. My friends used to be so different. Now all they do is hurt themselves and others.

"Clara Clam doesn't care about others any more. Sally Seahorse won't share. Craig and Carl Crab are fighting. Serena Shrimp is acting disrespectful. Marissa Manta doesn't trust her friend. The oysters aren't being tolerant. Elmer Eel is dishonest, and Larry Lobster has become irresponsible. I finally just gave up and came home," explained Ocho.

"Well, giving up won't solve the problem. Don't you know that? If you want something changed, you have to get out there and change it," said Ozzie.

"I know, but I just don't know how to change things," Ocho replied. "I know the way the sea creatures are behaving is wrong, but I don't know what to do about it."

"You know," replied Ozzie, "sometimes people get so used to things being okay that they forget it takes work to keep them that way. Maybe that's what happened in your sea community. Take Larry Lobster, for example. He was so used to the animals appreciating what he did that he began to take for granted that they would always be that way. And that's not the way it works. A responsible animal has to work at being responsible at all times. It's not something that is automatic."

"Your right, Ozzie, and it would be the same for all the animals. If they want to keep their good habits, they have to think about what they're doing at all times," answered Ocho.

"And another thing," continued Ozzie. "They need to realize that when things don't go their way, they can't give up. Like Marissa Manta. Her friend lied to her, and Marissa was hurt and disappointed. Instead of working her problem out, she let her hurt and disappointed feelings take over."

"I think we're on the right track, Ozzie, but what can we do?" asked Ocho.

"Let's put our heads together and see what we can come up with," suggested Ozzie.

Ozzie and Ocho talked about all the things that had gone wrong in the sea community. And before Ozzie left, Ocho had a plan.

MAR★CO PRODUCTS, INC. © 2002 1-800-448-2197

The next morning, Ocho set out to change the sea community back into the happy and thoughtful place it had once been. First, he came upon Clara Clam. There she was, still in the same place with her shell snapped shut. "Clara, it's me, Ocho! Open up your shell," called Ocho.

"Go away, Ocho! I don't want to see you or anyone else," answered Clara Clam.

"I'm not going to go away, Clara. And if you don't come out, I will cover both of us with an ink cloud," said Ocho.

Clara knew what that meant. When an octopus feels threatened, it often tries to escape by releasing a cloud of purple-black ink to confuse its enemies. This is a good trick if the octopus can quickly escape through the cloud. If the octopus can't escape, it will become sick and may die.

"You can't do that. It's too dangerous," warned Clara. "And besides, I'm not your enemy."

"I can do it, and I will," answered Ocho. "I would rather be sick than see you living the way you are." Ocho waited and waited. He was just about to give up when he saw Clara's shell opening.

"All right, you win. I don't want you to get hurt. But I don't want you to try and change me, either," said Clara.

MAR⋆CO PRODUCTS, INC. © 2002 1-800-448-2197

"I don't want to change you," said Ocho. "I just want you to be the same type of clam that you used to be."

"And how do you propose to do that?" Clara asked defiantly.

"Well, I have eight tentacles," said Ocho, "and each of them stands for something good. They are also magic," explained Ocho.

"Right," said Clara, in a tone of voice that expressed her disbelief.

"Come on! Give it a try. You've got nothing to lose," pleaded Ocho.

"Well, what do you want me to do?" asked Clara.

"I want you to look me straight in the eye and concentrate on what I am going to say to you. As you are doing that, I am going to touch your shell with my special tentacle," explained Ocho.

"What special tentacle?" asked Clara.

"The special tentacle that stands for *caring*. When you look me straight in the eye and I touch you with my special *caring* tentacle, you will again become the caring clam that you used to be. You will be ready to help others again, and our sea community will be like it was before—a wonderful place to live," Ocho promised.

"Are you sure?" asked Clara. "This sounds kind of strange to me."

"You have to believe," said Ocho.

Ocho told Clara to look directly into his eye. Then he carefully put one of his tentacles on Clara's shell. Holding his tentacle on her shell, he said:

It's very strange

To live in the sea

If creatures

Have no harmony.

So from this day forth,

It will be my quest

To help my friends

And do my best.

Ocho repeated the verse two more times. When he finished, he removed his tentacle from Clara's shell.

"Clara, from now on, you will be as you were before—a caring clam. No more will you reject sea creatures who need your help. If, for some reason, a sea creature doesn't act the same way toward you, you will remember that it is worth every effort you have to be a caring clam. Because if *you* are always caring, others will become caring, too. And even those who don't become caring right away will eventually learn from your actions and become caring, too," said Ocho.

Clara looked at Ocho. Her shell was open wide, and Ocho was overjoyed to see her expression.

"I hated not listening to others and helping if I could," Clara told him. "I don't know why I got so upset. I've always believed that if I was good and kind, others would be, too. And when they were not, I just forgot everything I believed in. From now on, I will remember that even though sea creatures will not always be caring toward me, most of the time they will. And I will always keep trying, no matter what happens. Thank you, Ocho. Your magic tentacle showed me how silly I was being."

When Clara finished talking, Ocho breathed a sign of relief. He knew that the sea community again had a caring clam who would be there to help sea creatures in distress.

"It worked! It really worked!" thought Ocho. "The plan Ozzie and I put together really worked. If it worked for Clara Clam, then maybe it will work for the others."

Ocho said good-bye to Clara.

Then Ocho crawled over to the beautiful plants where he had seen Sally Seahorse. Once he found Sally there, he told her the same thing he had told Clara. He told Sally about his special tentacle. But this tentacle was a *different* tentacle.

This tentacle stood for **sharing**. Ocho also told Sally that if she didn't listen to what he had to say, he would cover them both with a cloud of ink. Sally didn't want the ink squirted on her and Ocho, either. So she let Ocho touch her with his magic tentacle as he said his magic verse three times. By the time Ocho had finished, Sally had relaxed. She was happy to be herself again.

"Not sharing made me angry at myself," Sally told Ocho. "I didn't like the seahorse I'd become. I'm really happy that you shared your magic tentacle with me. It made me realize that if I'm happy when someone shares with me, then others will be happy when I share with them."

Ocho was amazed. The plan was working! The sea community was a better place because Sally Seahorse, who always shared with everyone, would show others how important it is to share.

Ocho said good-bye to Sally.

MAR★CO PRODUCTS, INC. © 2002 1-800-448-2197

Then Ocho crawled off to where he had seen Craig and Carl Crab fighting. They were still arguing. Ocho again explained what he would do and the crabs, like the seahorse and the clam, agreed it would be better to be touched by Ocho's magic tentacle than covered with the inky cloud.

Ocho told them that when he touched them with his tentacle that stood for being **cooperative**, they would again cooperate with each other and stop fighting.

The two crabs looked at each other and almost burst out laughing. It seemed like such a silly plan that they almost forgot about their own arguing. But Ocho ignored their doubts, touched them with his tentacle that stood for being **cooperative**, and recited his verse. As Ocho chanted, Craig and Carl became more serious. As soon as Ocho finished, Craig and Carl both began to apologize at once. This set them both to laughing, and Ocho told them how happy he was that they were going to cooperate with each other again. He added that their behavior would help the entire sea community see how important it is to cooperate with one other.

Ocho had eight tentacles. Each one stood for something different. He had already used his tentacles that stood for **sharing**, **caring**, and being **cooperative**. Now it was time to visit the other sea creatures and touch them with his other tentacles.

When Ocho reached Serena Shrimp, he touched her with the tentacle that stood for acting **respectful**, and she stopped talking back to her mother.

Marissa Manta was touched with the tentacle that stood for being **trustworthy**, and she and Mandy Manta talked with each other and became friends again.

The oysters were touched with the tentacle that stood for acting **tolerant**, and the little oyster and little mussel played happily together.

Ocho touched Elmer Eel with the tentacle that stood for being **honest**, and Elmer returned the gold chain to Eleanor.

🐟 **24** 🐟

MAR★CO PRODUCTS, INC. © 2002 1-800-448-2197

Now it was time to face Larry Lobster. Ocho crawled over to Larry's house. It was still a mess. "Larry," called Ocho. "I have a surprise for you."

"What's that?" asked Larry.

"Well, you won't believe it, but all of the sea creatures in your community are back to being their old selves."

"So what?" answered Larry.

"So what? So that means you can go back to being in charge and you will feel appreciated," replied Ocho.

"I don't know," Larry said. "I'm not sure I *want* to go back to being in charge. Let someone else be responsible. I'd just as soon sit here and be uninvolved."

"Oh, no!" thought Ocho. "Do I have to prove how important responsibility is to Larry Lobster like I had to prove how important the other character traits are to the other sea creatures?"

Larry just looked at Ocho, so Ocho went into action. Ocho gave Larry the same speech that he'd given the other sea creatures. Larry didn't want to be sprayed with ink any more than the others had, so he went along with Ocho's plan. Ocho had one special tentacle left, the tentacle that stood for acting **responsible**. He touched Larry with this special tentacle, and recited his verses. It worked like it had before.

When Ocho finished his chant, Larry looked at his house and said, "What a mess! I can't live like this! I'll get everything in order as soon as I get back from visiting the other sea creatures in our community. I need to let them know that I'm back on the job and will be doing what is expected of me."

Ocho crawled back to his cave. He was now a happy octopus. Ozzie was waiting for him.

"Did it work?" Ozzie asked anxiously.

"It was a cinch!" Ocho announced proudly. The two octopuses gave a tentacle high five, and Ozzie went back to his community.

Meanwhile, Larry Lobster sat on his rock, chuckling to himself. "That Ocho!" he thought. "Special tentacles? I don't think so! Ocho was just smart enough to think of a way to get all of us back to being what we wanted to be all along."

DISCUSSION QUESTIONS PERTAINING TO CHAPTER I

1. Why was Ocho worried about his sea community? *(He was worried because the sea creatures had changed their behavior and were no longer concerned about others.)*

2. Why did Clara Clam stop caring about others? *(She felt she always listened to the problems of others, but no one cared enough to listen to her problems.)*

3. Why didn't the oysters want the mussel in their oyster bed? *(The mussel was different from them and they didn't want anything different in their community.)*

4. How did Ocho know that Serena Shrimp was disrespectful? *(She was talking back to her mother.)*

5. Why didn't Larry Lobster want to be responsible? *(He felt he wasn't appreciated.)*

DISCUSSION QUESTIONS PERTAINING TO CHAPTER II

6. What was the plan that Ozzie and Ocho worked out? *(They decided to tell the sea creatures that Ocho had special tentacles that would help them change their behavior back to what it had been.)*

7. Why did the sea creatures let Ocho touch them with his special tentacles? *(Ocho said that if they didn't let him touch them with his special tentacles, he would spray himself and them with a special type of ink. The sea creatures knew this was dangerous for Ocho and could make him sick or even kill him. They didn't want this to happen to Ocho, so they went along with what he wanted to do.)*

8. Did Ocho have special tentacles? *(Not really. Saying that he did was just a way to get the sea creatures to think about what they were doing.)*

9. Why did Ocho's plan work? *(It worked because the sea creatures really wanted to behave as they had before and Ocho's plan made them realize this.)*

FOLLOW-UP ACTIVITIES

CHARACTER WORDMAN: Tell the students that they are to find other words that mean the same thing as the character traits in the story. Explain that it is their task to guess the word before the entire figure is drawn on the board or overhead transparency. Draw a line for each letter in the word you wish the students to discover. For example, if the word is *considerate*, draw:

— — — — — — — — — — —

Then tell the students that you are looking for a word that means *caring*. Divide the students into two or more teams. Go from one team to another, allowing each team one turn to guess a letter. If the letter guessed is in the word, place it on the appropriate line. If the letter guessed is *not* in the word, draw a part of the *wordman*, starting with the head and moving down toward the feet. The team that guesses the word wins a point, and the team with the most points wins the game.

Here are some suggested words:

Caring	considerate, thoughtful, concerned
Responsible	dependable, trustworthy, accountable
Cooperative	give-and-take, working together, collaboration
Honest	truthful, trustworthy, sincere
Trustworthy	reliable, loyal, faithful
Tolerant	accepting, impartial, just
Sharing	unselfish, generous, benevolent
Respectful	courteous, considerate, honorable

TIC-TAC CHARACTER: Draw a tic-tac-toe game on the board or overhead transparency. Divide the students into two teams, Team A and Team B. Tell the students that you will ask Team A a question. If they answer correctly, either and "X" or an "O" will be placed on the empty square of their choice. Then you will ask Team B a question and repeat the process. The first team to get three "X's" or "O's" in a row wins the game.

Tic-Tac Character Questions: (All answers are either true or false.)

1. A student who steals is dishonest. *True*
2. When students work together, they are cooperative. *True*
3. A student who does not return a borrowed item is responsible. *False*
4. A student who is not interested in someone's problem is not caring. *True*
5. A student who is not charged for an item in a store and who says nothing about it is honest. *False*
6. A student who keeps all her toys to herself is not a student who shares. *True.*
7. A student who puts others down because of their race is tolerant. *False*
8. A student who can keep a secret is trustworthy. *True*
9. A student who helps a wounded bird is caring. *True*
10. A student who talks back to his parents is respectful. *False*
11. A student who includes everyone in a game, even if they can't play well, is tolerant. *True*
12. A student who frequently forgets his lunch money is responsible. *False*
13. A student who breaks a promise is not trustworthy. *True*
14. A student who listens to the opinions of others is respectful. *True*
15. A student who plays her best in a team game is cooperative. *True*
16. A student who offers a pencil to a student who doesn't have one is sharing. *True*
17. A student who runs through a neighbor's flower beds is respectful. *False*
18. A student who breaks a window and says he didn't do it is honest. *False*
19. A student who never has time to listen to another student's problems is caring. *False*
20. A student who always does his homework is responsible. *True*
21. A student who has to have her own way is not cooperative. *True*
22. A student who refuses to play with a student who is slower than the rest of the players is tolerant. *False*
23. A student who does what he says he will do is trustworthy. *True*
24. A student who has a bag of peanuts and eats them in front of her friends is not a sharing student. *True*

SEA CREATURE CHARACTER TRAITS

The sea creatures in Ocho's community had eight different character traits. When each of them used these traits, the community was a peaceful place to live. Draw a line from the character trait to the sea creature to whom it belongs.

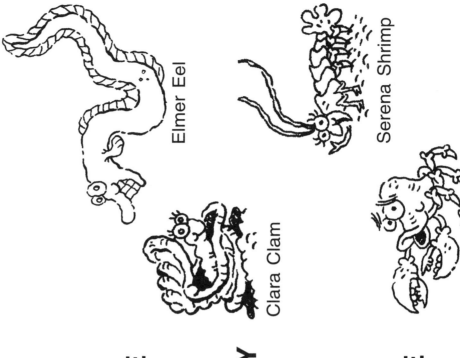

Elmer Eel

Serena Shrimp

Clara Clam

Carl Crab

SHARING

RESPONSIBLE

CARING

TRUSTWORTHY

HONEST

RESPECTFUL

COOPERATIVE

TOLERANT

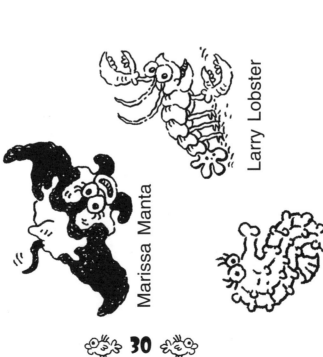

Marissa Manta

Larry Lobster

Oyster

Sally Seahorse

30

OCHO'S SPECIAL TENTACLES

Write a character trait from the story on each tentacle. Then color your picture. Place your finished picture in a spot where it will remind you to practice the character traits.

OCHO'S WORD FIND

Find the hidden words.

```
E  M  O  I  B  C  A  R  G  W  L  R
N  C  O  O  P  E  R  A  T  I  V  E
S  H  A  R  I  N  G  K  B  F  R  S
T  O  S  R  J  Y  U  O  M  V  X  P
O  P  D  H  I  K  T  D  N  C  H  E
L  W  B  L  A  N  O  F  I  A  O  C
E  Z  B  M  O  W  G  Q  R  P  N  T
R  E  S  P  O  N  S  I  B  L  E  F
A  W  I  N  V  M  C  L  N  C  S  U
N  P  E  X  B  Y  A  S  M  G  T  L
T  R  U  S  T  W  O  R  T  H  Y  R
C  S  W  Y  I  P  L  M  A  B  T  E
```

CARING   RESPONSIBLE
COOPERATIVE   SHARING
HONEST   TOLERANT
RESPECTFUL   TRUSTWORTHY

MAR★CO PRODUCTS, INC. © 2002 1-800-448-2197